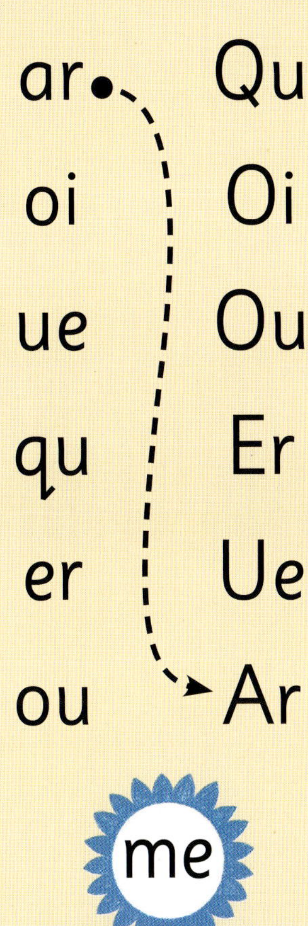

me
we
be

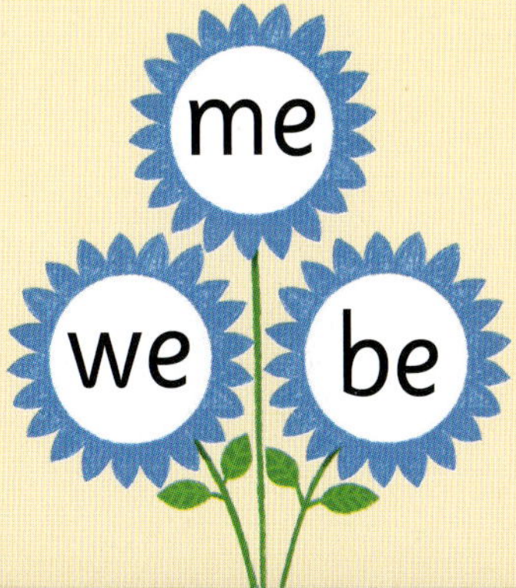

Granddad is in the attic.

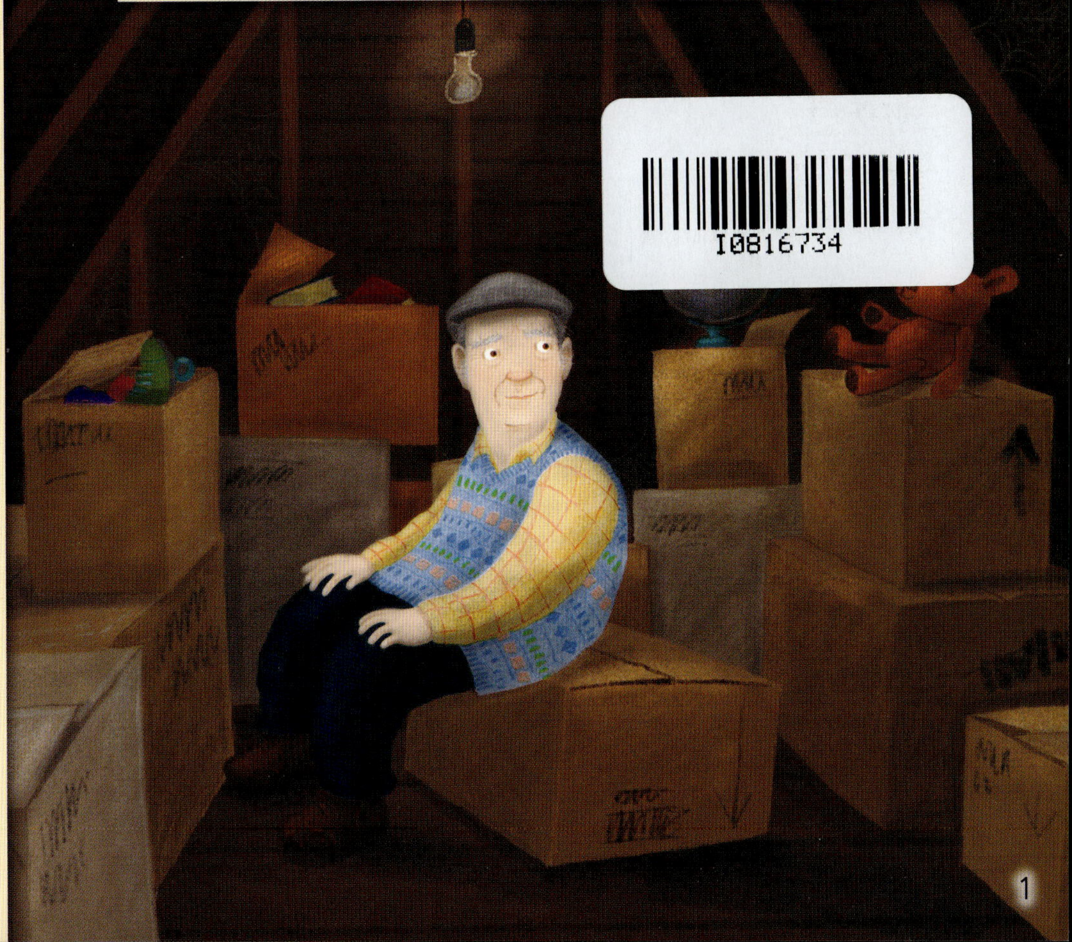

He is looking for his oil lamp.

It must be in a box...
...but which box?

Scarlett and Quentin can look, too.

Atishoo!
It must be the dust. Have a tissue.

I am an explorer on a quest.

It is dark in the attic.

Granddad and Quentin have
still not found the oil lamp.

Then, from the gloom...
Boo!

Help me, Granddad!
It's a monster!

It's not a monster! It's me, Scarlett.

Scarlett has found the oil lamp!